When Snow Lay Soft on the Mountain

by Patricia Hermes Illustrated by Leslie Baker

LITTLE, BROWN AND COMPANY
Boston New York Toronto London

First Edition

Library of Congress Cataloging-in-Publication Data

Hermes, Patricia.
When snow lay soft on the mountain / by Patricia Hermes ; illustrated by Leslie Baker. — 1st ed.
p. cm.
Summary: Through the changing seasons on Hairy Bear Mountain and her father's illness, Hallie continues to wish for her father's health and a china doll's head from a store window in town.
ISBN 0-316-36005-8
[1. Fathers and daughters — Fiction. 2. Wishes — Fiction. 3. Dolls — Fiction. 4. Mountain life — Fiction.] I. Baker, Leslie A., ill. II. Title.
PZ7.H4317Whj 1996
[Fic] — dc20 95-18323

10 9 8 7 6 5 4 3 2 1

WOR

Published simultaneously in Canada by Little, Brown & Company (Canada) Limited

Printed in the United States of America

The paintings in this book were done in watercolors on Strathmore Bristol paper.

FOR JESSICA AND SAM

—P. H.

FOR MARIA MODUGNO

—L. B.

ON NIGHTS WHEN THE MOONLIGHT lay soft on the mountain, nights when spring was so close that Hallie could feel its breath in her hair, she and Papa would walk out on Hairy Bear Mountain. Above them, stars hung so low they seemed to tangle in the branches of the cottonwood tree. After they had walked far enough, Papa would point out the secrets of spring on the mountain.

They'd kneel in the damp, rich earth, and parting some fallen leaves, Papa would find the star flowers that bloom only by moonlight. Once, on a particularly bright night, he spotted a deer. It pawed at the ground and shook its fierce head as though daring the moon to come down and play. One spring night, his sharp mountain eyes picked out coyote pups as they tumbled and played in and out of the moon shadows.

If the night was particularly mild, Hallie and Papa would go farther up the mountain, to the stream that rushed down from the peaks and rumbled over stones, rolling them smooth as it went. Hallie would then pluck a stone from the tumbling water to wish upon and carry back down the mountain. Holding that snow-cold stone, she could tell that winter still held sway at the top of the mountain. Later, Hallie would add her wishing stone to the others that lined the path by their mountain home.

As they turned homeward, it would be Hallie's time to talk. Papa would ask about her latest wish — for Hallie gathered wishes the way the cottonwood gathered stars.

Hallie would tell Papa how she wished for snow in summer, and in winter, for blackberries. At Christmas, she always wished for two oranges, one for herself and one to give to Aunt Belle. Hallie wished that the quilts Aunt Belle made and sold in Grover's store would bring ten dollars each.

Once in a while, come time for Hallie's birthday in March, she wished for a new dress, but not often, for she knew that new dresses were even harder to come by than blackberries in winter.

Sometimes Hallie's wishes were granted. (And how did Papa find oranges in winter?) Mostly they were not, for not even Papa could work miracles, although Hallie knew he would if he could. So she kept one wish a secret, all to herself, knowing Papa would grieve if he could not grant this wish. Hallie wished for a doll. No, not even a doll — just a china doll's head.

Five of them had been placed in the window of Grover's store, and one of them seemed to call to Hallie, to beckon her heart. Its hair was soft like a real baby's, and its mouth was curved and sweet. But everything in Grover's store cost money, money that Papa did not have. Besides, Hallie knew, a doll's head needed a body, a body that only a mama knew how to sew. But Hallie's mama had died when Hallie was still a baby.

Hallie named the doll Avery and pretended it belonged to her although it had to live in the store window. Hallie knew that living in a store window would be lonely, so each time she went to town, she would stop by the window and say good morning to Avery. And on the way home, she would stop and say good night.

Winter came early to the mountain that year. Before Thanksgiving was past, the snows had come, drifting to the top of Hallie and Papa's home, blocking off windows. It became so dark inside that they could barely see the checkers spread out in front of them. Then came the influenza that carried off so many neighbors to lie beside Mama in the graveyard. Papa, too, fell ill and lay feverish in his bed, unable to speak for the coughing. Hallie did the best she could to care for him. When it was not enough, she went to town for Aunt Belle.

Aunt Belle brought medicines and a special quilt for Papa and settled in with Hallie. Snow again came softly to the mountain, as Papa tossed feverishly on his bed.

As Christmas approached, Hallie walked out on the mountain path alone. There, among the snow-covered wishing stones, she stood and thought about Papa. And she thought about her wishes and about Avery, her doll. She knew she couldn't have Avery for herself, with Papa so sick. But oh, she wished Avery wasn't as lonely as she.

Nights on the mountain became colder and longer as Christmas approached, a Christmas without dreams or wishes. And on Christmas morning, there were no oranges.

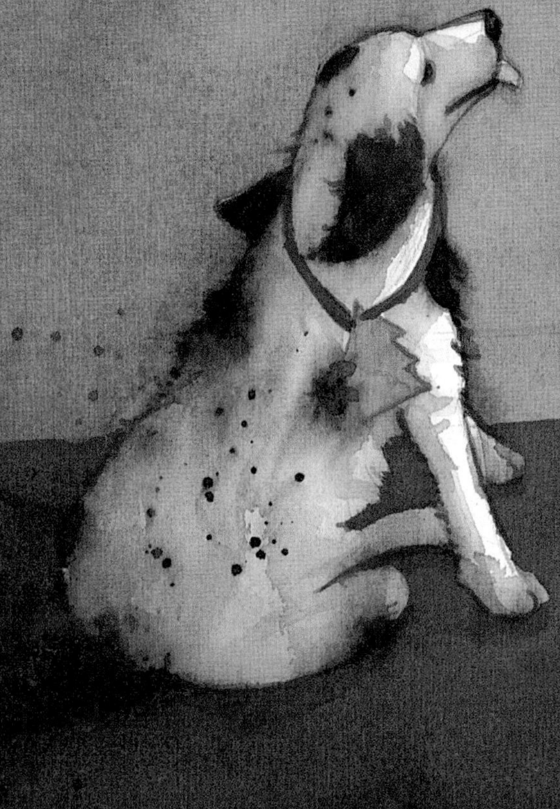

December gave way to January and January to February, and winter once again was melting into spring. Papa didn't cough so much, although he still lay in his bed. Some days Hallie even thought she heard him whisper to Aunt Belle. Without Papa to walk with her on the mountain, though, Hallie closed her eyes and ears to the coming spring, to the blooming of the cottonwood tree, to the rumbling of the stream high above, to the coyote pups tumbling in and out of moon shadows. But try as she might, she could not close her heart to her secret wish.

And then, one warm March morning when she awoke, there on her bed was Avery.

No, it could not be Avery, this softly stuffed, beautiful doll. Avery lived in Grover's store.

Hallie closed her eyes.

Dreaming, that's what she was doing. She kept her eyes closed, pretending to herself that she was sleeping. Then slowly she pretended to wake herself and again slowly opened her eyes.

Avery was still there. Avery with the real hair and the mouth that smiled at Hallie and beckoned her heart. Avery wearing a blue checked dress and wrapped in a brightly patterned quilt.

Hallie snatched Avery to her and held her close, Avery's soft woolen body warming quickly to her own.

"They knew!" Hallie whispered to Avery. "Papa and Aunt Belle. They knew my secret wish!"

Then, holding Avery tightly, Hallie ran to see Aunt Belle and Papa.

Aunt Belle just nodded. Papa was strong enough to take Hallie's hand and hold it tightly and to whisper, "Happy birthday."

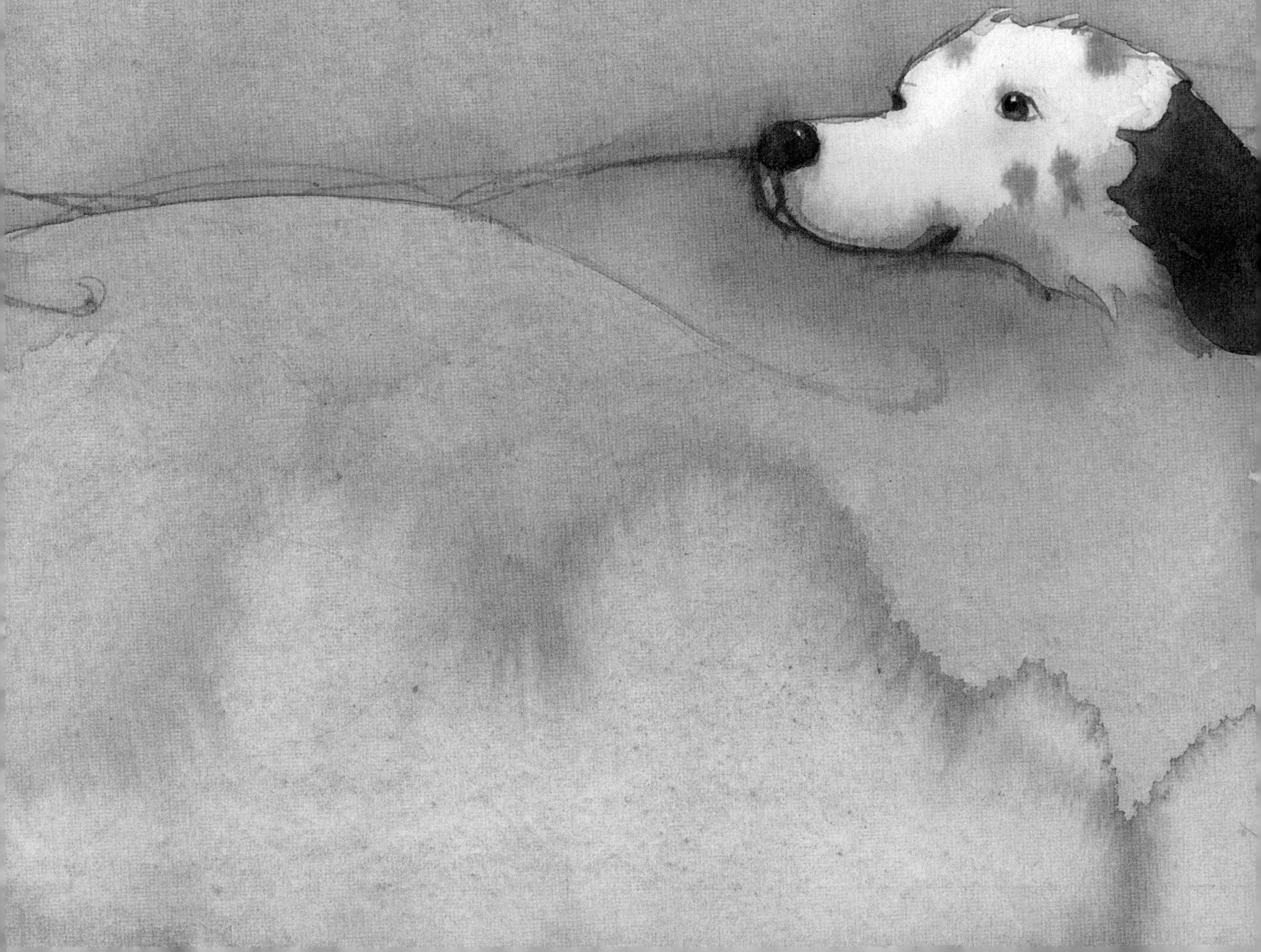

That night, as spring lay soft on the mountain, as the stars hung so low they seemed to tangle in the branches of the cottonwood tree, Hallie and Papa took Avery walking on Hairy Bear Mountain — not far, just to the wishing stone path, for Papa was still weak. Hallie showed Avery the deer that crept down from the mountain, pointed out to her the star flowers that bloomed only by moonlight. She turned Avery's face up and showed her the stars and told her about the rumbling stream up on the mountain, things Avery had never imagined in her life in the store window.

Then, as they turned back home, Hallie holding Papa's arm, she told Avery it was her turn to talk, to tell Hallie about her wishes. Although Avery didn't speak — not loud, anyway — Hallie knew that dolls had wishes. She knew that dolls wished to come live with a little girl. And both she and Avery knew then that even the most impossible wishes sometimes come true.